FIDDL: MISSING

For Brad:
Be brave & Shine on!

BY DONNA REID

Donna Reid

Dedicated to my grandchildren.
I will always hold you safely in my heart.

Love,
Grandma Donna

All images remixed with the help of Canva AI by Studio Dreamshare Press, with book design and layout by Rose Bennett.

For permissions or other inquiries, contact:
studiodreamshare@gmail.com

@StudioDreamsharePress
www.studiodreamsharepress.com
ISBN: 978-1-989832-09-7

1

Although Twyla was only as big as a second, Grandma Fannie told her that she had more gumption than the tallest, loudest creature in Bugcroft, and even the whole Fantasy Forest.

"Twyla May Firefly, just because your middle name ends in a 'Y', doesn't mean you have to question everything!" Grandma Fannie said. "You sure don't need any encouragement when it comes to learning new things or conjuring up ways to figure out the answers to all your questions."

Twyla's brain started buzzing when she held a question in her mind. She started vibrating and thought she could almost hear herself hum.

Thought: *I look like one of those sparkly things the children from the farm light on special occasions.*

Thought: *Ooooops! I'd better not let Grandma Fannie hear me say that… she would be very upset if she knew I flew past the Bugcroft town limit!*

Thought: *She says it isn't safe.*

Thought: *Why isn't it safe?*

Now she was really starting to shine. Twyla closed her eyes tight, pulled in her bottom lip, and willed her little butt to light up.

"Here I glow," she squeaked. She knew she was heading into question mode when the glow cast enough light that she could use it to see where to fly.

I'm sure glad I don't need batteries, just questions, she thought.

"My last name should be Fireworks, not Firefly!" she chirped, twirling for effect, all aglow. She zoomed into the kitchen.

How convenient is this? What's in here? she wondered as she opened the cupboard door.

Twyla loved the way Grandma Fannie's kitchen smelled. It was one of the reasons she spent so much time here.

Oooh, I wonder what kind of yummy treats Grandma Fannie made today? she thought.

As she flitted around Grandma Fannie's kitchen, her

mind went from question to question. She couldn't contain her thoughts. She wondered about big issues that were going on beyond her tiny town limits, like *how come the carrots that grow in the Family Farm are orange? How do the trees in Fantasy Forest know when to turn colour in the fall?*

As she grew tired her thoughts began to focus on smaller issues. *Wonder what I will do tomorrow? Will Fiddle come by to visit? How come I haven't seen them in a while? Did they go on an adventure without me?*

She knew that this was very unlikely, but she was really starting to wonder why she hadn't heard from her favourite cousin, Fiddle.

Twyla landed on the kitchen stool and Grandma could see the glow from the corner of her eye as she stirred the pot of cream-of-cricket soup over the fire.

"Where is she going with this?" muttered Grandma. She didn't look up as she cautioned, "I worry where your curiosity will take you next!"

Grandma Fannie sounded stern but she couldn't help but smile as she thought how very much like herself her little granddaughter was. She didn't even have to turn around to know that Twyla was in full glow mode and probably not hearing a word she was saying.

Twyla could admit that her curiosity got her into a bit of trouble now and then. She went on many adventures with her cousin Fiddle, because if they got in really big trouble one of them could go for help. Twyla and Fiddle were usually inseparable, and got along like two peas in a pod... or two flies in a jar, the night that Larry Ladybug caught them spying on him. She would never forget that time.

Twyla and Fiddle were searching for amusement that evening. They camouflaged themselves with blades of grass and the petals from a daisy, but the disguise didn't keep their voices from carrying from behind the fence, across the yard to where Larry Ladybug was practicing his walk for his big night. Larry couldn't see them, but he heard them whispering and giggling. He sighed and chose to ignore them and continued getting ready for the annual charity ball.

"Am I wrong to want to win the award for Most Charitable Citizen of Bugcroft again this year?" he wondered. "I try to be as humble as a bug can be, but giving is so rewarding and the more I give the more I should be rewarded!" He blushed. "Well, who's gonna toot my horn if I don't do it myself?"

He draped a floppy dandelion leaf over his shoulders and applied fluffy white seeds to his eyelashes to enhance his beauty. He looked at himself in the reflection of a candy wrapper, and struck a dramatic pose.

Twyla and Fiddle watched from their hiding place.

Fiddle in particular was transfixed. They were mesmerized by Larry Ladybug's transformation from a simple beetle into a lovely queenly bug.

"Oooh la la," whispered Twyla to Fiddle. They both burst into excited giggles and rolled around in their hiding spot.

"Hey! I know you're hiding in there!" Larry Ladybug yelled with a sharp look in their direction. The giggling increased, and Twyla and Fiddle's glow-butts started to shine, giving them away. Larry rolled his eyes.

Nosy little fireflies, he grumbled, applying blackberry lipstick to complete his look.

Fiddle longed to try on Larry Ladybug's collection of high heels and milkweed wigs and pose in the candy wrapper mirror. That would be fun!

Larry rearranged the emerald green leaf on his shoulders and stood up straighter, admiring the curve of his cheek. Larry was so happy with who he was. The fireflies giggled harder.

"Ladybug, Lordybug, what's the difference?" said Larry.

The bugs in Bugcroft knew him and loved him, but sometimes bugs from places that were not so kind tried to dampen his self-esteem.

He was a proud bug, and he would not let those silly fireflies spoil his special day. He paraded up and down his short makeshift runway with his chest puffed out and his hand on his hip.

Fiddle burst into applause, joined by Twyla.

"Bravo!" they said with genuine admiration.

The fireflies cheered. Larry Ladybug took a deep bow, and flew off into the forest to gather fresh pollen for his eye shadow.

Twyla and Fiddle didn't notice that they had rolled to the edge of the fencepost. Suddenly, they tumbled down, down... into an old glass jar. The jar tipped over, trapping them inside.

Round and round the jar they flew, their panic growing.

"If we hadn't been laughing so hard, we might have stood a chance," said Fiddle. "What are we going to do?"

"Don't worry, Fiddle, Larry will be back after the charity ball and he'll help us out of here... I hope," said Twyla.

They flew round and round and round.

Suddenly they saw the bright gossamer wings of Beatrice Butterfly. Beatrice looked down at the glowing bugs in the jar for a moment and then took off.

"There's Beatrice Butterfly!" said Fiddle.

"She's spying on us," said Twyla. "Her last name

should be Butting-fly, not Butterfly! She's always butting in. I bet she's on her way to tell someone as fast as her wings will take her. I wonder who she'll tell."

Twyla slumped down in the bottom of the jar beside Fiddle, and they hugged tightly while they awaited their fate.

Sure enough, Beatrice, more of a no-nonsense type, was quick to report to Twyla's Grandma Fannie. She knew that Fannie was always worried about Twyla's safety. Like others in Bugcroft, Beatrice had heard Fannie trying to tell Twyla more than once that her escapades were setting her up for trouble.

Grandma Fannie's brow would scrunch together, and she would lean in to make eye contact with Twyla to make sure she had her attention. She would wag her finger gently in front of Twyla's nose to stress the importance of what she was saying, take a deep breath and then say, "Twyla May Firefly, a good little firefly would not go rushing into danger just to satisfy her curiosity!"

She would raise her voice just a bit and lean in a little closer before she would finish with "Oh Twyla, your behavior is the fright of me!"

Later, she would say "I know how important it is for you to find answers to all of your questions, but please, please be more cautious. I love you far too much for anything to ever happen to you. Do you understand?"

Twyla always nodded her head but crossed her fingers behind her shimmering back.

Grandma Fannie was not surprised when Beatrice came beating her wings at the door. Beatrice didn't care if she was tattling or not, and her words came tumbling out as fast as the white-water rapids on the Rambling River.

"They're in a jar! Trapped! Not much air, I'm sure! They were spying! No, not me, no never, ever. I was certainly not spying, I was only watching them because they were being nosy! Not me, no never, ever! I would never spy unless it was necessary!"

Fannie took a deep breath in hopes that Beatrice would do the same.

"They can't breathe! Torture them! He will! Larry! With a pair of rusty eyebrow tweezers from the community recycle pile, for spying on him!"

At this point, Grandma Fannie put up her hand and commanded Beatrice to STOP.

"Please, take a breath! You aren't making any sense so just calm down."

Grandma Fannie knew about Beatrice Butterfly's flare for exaggeration, and that Larry Ladybug was not capable of doing anything mean to anyone. She also knew that anything was possible when Twyla was out and about with her cousin Fiddle. She patted Beatrice on the hand while the butterfly tried to regain her composure.

"Larry caught Twyla and Fiddle spying on him in his backyard. He has them in a jar, and I think he is going to use them for a lamp to light up the runway at the award ceremony later tonight."

Grandma Fannie's eyebrow was arched in a way that showed she really didn't believe the butterfly's tall tale.

"It's the truth!" said Beatrice, something she insisted often when bugs were skeptical. "Please come and help them!"

That was all Grandma Fannie needed to hear before she untied her apron, hung it on the hook by the door and grabbed her hat.

Whether Beatrice is telling a tall tale or not, she thought, *I have to go and make sure those little bugs are safe.*

This was not the first time she had to go after them, and it surely would not be the last.

Déjà vu" she sighed. "Why can't those two just go and play like other bugs?"

Grandma Fannie flew off after Beatrice Butterfly.

"Here we go again..." she said.

2

By the time Beatrice led Grandma Fannie to the scene of the crime, Larry had not only helped the cousins from the jar, but the two were now his captivated audience as he finished completing his look for the charity ball. A few minor adjustments and he was ready for a real runway! With his neatly applied eyelashes stretching out from his already lengthy natural ones, he batted his way across the stage. He looked brilliant enough with his colourful red coat, but the dandelion leaf shrug provided the right pop of colour that would make any lordy or lady bug's head turn. Larry was soaking up the attention as Twyla and Fiddle whistled and applauded his latest collection.

All three had forgotten the jar incident when Fannie cleared her throat to make her presence known. They gasped as she stood with hand on hip and they knew right away that Beatrice, who was fluttering behind her, had ratted them out. Fannie didn't know whether to be relieved or angry when she saw them having so much fun. She also didn't know if she should be angry at Beatrice, or at the curious cousins, or at Larry, even though he had the biggest heart of anyone in the Forest, and Beatrice was a shameless spreader of tall tales.

Grandma Fannie cleared her throat again to give herself time to calm down and let her blood pressure get back to normal. This was something she had practiced, since Twyla was her granddaughter.

"Well," she started, turning to Beatrice Butterfly. "Things don't seem quite as bad as you explained to me".

Beatrice blushed and started to explain that the fireflies were indeed in the jar when she fled for help.

"They were in there! Honest! See, there's the jar with their wing prints all over the inside of it!"

Her voice trailed off when she realized she was wasting her time. How dare they sit there with their big wide grins! They got her in trouble this time without even doing anything!

Maybe, Beatrice thought, *I will just leave them to their own devices next time… and with these two flies, there will be a next time.*

The more Beatrice thought about the predicament the more worked up she got. *Maybe I did get in a bit of a flap when I started to tell Grandma Fannie what was going on...*

She admitted to herself that she felt jealous of the fireflies because it always seemed like they were having fun, even when they appeared to be in trouble. How was this possible?

"Those darn bugs could fall in a pile of compost and still come out smelling like roses!" she exclaimed as she left in a huff.

"I know Mama will believe me," muttered Beatrice as she flew away home.

Maybe I need to lighten up, she thought, *but I don't think I could ever be as brave as a firefly. I will never be able to shine like them. It isn't fair,* she pouted. *The Fireflies look like fire. I'm a butterfly but I don't look like butter. I try so hard to just be myself...*

She recalled her mother telling her that her beauty was in the shape of her wings. "Beatrice Butterfly, your wings were fashioned after an angel harp."

Beatrice saw the resemblance when she was feeling confident enough to look at her reflection in the river.

"I am a beautiful butterfly", she smiled for the first time since the drama began. "Never mind those silly fireflies, I love being a butterfly!"

She knew that even though the day went a bit haywire, and she had turned her version of the jar event into a juicy bit of gossip for Twyla's Grandma Fannie, she really did have the best interests of the little fireflies at heart.

Grandma Fannie snorted. *Butterflies are so dramatic,* she thought. She remembered how Beatrice's aunts would carry on in the Bugcroft school.

She turned to Larry Ladybug.

"Sorry for these two little interlopers," she said, looking sternly at Twyla and Fiddle.

The cousins looked at each other and tried not to giggle.

"They sure are curious," he said, with a pointed look.

"Thanks for helping them out of a sticky situation, Larry. It's hard for me to keep track of them and it's great to know that we live in a community where everyone watches out for everyone else, even perhaps a little too closely... You've got my vote for the Most Charitable Citizen of the Year again this year," said Grandma Fannie.

"I appreciate your vote, my friend," said Larry. "I know the little ones meant no harm."

Larry turned to Fiddle and Twyla.

"Now off with the two of you, I have to finish getting

ready! Shoo fly!" He jokingly made a shooing gesture.

"Come, NOW," said Grandma Fannie. She continued to share her life lessons with Twyla and Fiddle on the way home from Larry's.

"Don't you roll your eyes at me now, Twyla," she snapped. Then she softened. "You know that this little adventure you had today could have had a horrible ending. You know you got off lucky this time. You really must start being more careful."

Twyla tried hard not to roll her eyes again, because it would just prolong the lecture.

"You know that you should listen to me," continued Grandma Fannie.

As always, her talk ended with the same question.

"Do you know how much I love you?"

They were almost home.

"Twyla? Twyla, are you listening?" Grandma Fannie snapped her wings in front of Twyla's nose.

"Yes, Grandma, I know, I know...you worry because you love me. I love you, too," she smiled. She didn't even have to tell her that she had been daydreaming. Grandma Fannie always seemed to know what was going on, almost like she could read her mind.

Back in the safety of Grandma Fannie's kitchen, Twyla sipped her cup of warm wintergreen berry tea and wondered why her grandmother was so stuffy. She loved her to bits and felt deeply loved, but she could not understand how they could be so different.

I have to look into this more on The World Wide Web, she thought. She wasn't sure which spider had created this particular web or how on earth it was able to connect her to so much information but she sure loved being able to search the internet for answers to all of her questions.

"Why are grandmas hard to explain?"

She often heard Grandma Fannie say "when I was a little fly..." but could not for the life of her imagine what that was like.

Twyla had looked through the dusty old photo albums a million times, but it was still hard to believe that her grandma was ever younger, let alone a kid. The stories she told about her youth were hard to believe, but they were very interesting, and Twyla could listen to her talk about the "good old days" forever. She loved snuggling in the blanket Grandma Fannie made and nibbling on a fresh batch of sugar-coated insect snacks that she had whipped up. They would clink their glasses of sparkling dew drops together and pretend that it was the finest champagne. There really was no safer feeling than curling up on their tiny couch. Grandma Fannie was not just good at lectures and kissing boo-boos; she was the best at making a little fly feel like the most loved one in the universe.

Twyla got up to go and brush her teeth in preparation for bed. She loved sleeping over at her grandparents'. The sun would be coming up soon and it was time for her to "hit the hay" as her grandma sometimes referred to bedtime. She would never for the life of her understand how some creatures stayed up all day and slept all night. It just didn't seem normal. What the heck was normal anyway? It was hard to get her brain to stop the questions at the end of the night. This was one of the topics that she and Fiddle spent hours talking about.

Twyla was really missing her cousin a lot. They had never been apart this long for as long as she could remember. She knew it would be difficult to fall asleep if she worried about Fiddle so she sent out positive thoughts to keep her cousin safe and decided that tomorrow they must get together for sure.

Fiddle is my best friend, she thought, *and Fiddle is also the best party planner in Bugcroft!*

Twyla and Fiddle were planning Grandma Fannie and Grandpa Fog's anniversary party.

They will be so surprised, she thought with a smile. *We have so much more planning to do…*

Just thinking of all there was to do for the party was enough to help Twyla fall asleep.

3

"Twyla... Twyla..." Grandma Fannie gently nudged Twyla awake. "It's time to get ready."

Twyla blinked sleepily.

"You don't want to get left behind, do you? Grandpa has been up for hours, and he might just leave without us if you don't hurry. You know how much he loves the Ramblin' River Bluegrass Festival!"

Twyla jumped out of bed giving her grandmother a big hug and hurried to get dressed.

"I'm so glad I get to go again this year, but I can't believe that Fiddle isn't coming with us," said Twyla.

"Are you sure Fiddle didn't leave a message? Why don't

you hurry and check your email one last time and maybe we can pick Fiddle up on the way," suggested Grandma Fannie. She tried not to let worry creep into her voice, but she agreed that it was odd they did not get a reply from Fiddle about attending the festival with them. It was a yearly event and they had been taking Twyla since she was knee high to a grasshopper. Fiddle wasn't always able to come with them but hadn't missed the last few years.

Twyla loved spending time with her grandparents and the Bluegrass Festival lasted the whole weekend. Her siblings didn't mind her not being around because they were always a bit worried that her curious behaviour was going to fly back and light them up too. They loved her but it didn't hurt to be a bit cautious. Twyla's baby sister Twinkle was quite happy to have her parents' attention to herself and her brother, Twitch was always busy building things with his toys or dancing. He hardly noticed when she was gone. Grandma and Grandpa didn't seem to have any problem devoting their full attention to ensuring her safety. They had lots of time now that they were retired and wouldn't give up looking after Twyla for anything.

Bluegrass was not Twyla's favourite kind of music, even though it was hard not to tap your toe when the instruments lit up. She preferred pop entertainers like

Bustin' Beaver and Ladybug A-Gogo. She hummed along as often as she could and dreamt of one day being a big star with thousands of fans. Grandma didn't seem to mind the newer music.

"It really doesn't matter what kind of music you listen to; all music is good for the soul," Grandma Fannie would say.

Grandpa Fog seemed offended by the popular songs.

"What the heck are the kids today talking about? I can't figure it out, for the life of me. Sounds like a bunch of bangin' to me," he would mutter.

Twyla thought that maybe her grandpa liked bluegrass so much because when the strings were being tickled, lyrics weren't even needed.

They loaded up Dusty, their patched-up Winnebago.

"She was a Hot Wheel in her day, but now she seems to do best on the downhill slide," Grandpa Fog remarked.

Part of the adventure was just getting there. Twyla was happy to be settled in the back seat but disappointed that Fiddle hadn't answered any of her messages and wasn't coming with them.

The compartment underneath Dusty the Winnebago was as full of parts as camping necessities.

"We sure are lucky you can fix anything, Grandpa," Twyla would say. "I'm glad you're so handy, I know you'll get us there and back, no problem."

It was good that the festivals were not too far from town, so even if the worst were to happen, they could fly home if they had to. It was more the ritual of packing up and camping that seemed to matter to the fans.

Twyla peered out the window as they pulled into the campground.

"I feel sad that Fiddle isn't here to see all the bright lights, but I know they would want me to have a great time..."

Her excitement was growing now that the campground was in sight, and she could hardly contain herself.

The R.V. lurched to a stop and Twyla almost flew off of the seat when it backfired.

POW!

She was relieved when Grandpa Fog turned off the engine and hoped the smoke from the back end would be mistaken for one of the many campfires that lit up the sky. Most of the vehicles nowadays were electric, and made no noise and no pollution.

"Whew! We made it!" she coughed and waved the air to fan away the fumes.

Grandpa Fog jumped out of the driver's seat and got caught up in the excitement too.

"Look!" he pointed. "There's Wanda Pincer, under the pine tree, jamming with The Earwigs."

"I sure hope the Goodness Brothers are here this year," said Grandma Fannie. "They are such good-lookin' fellows and boy can they sing great harmony!"

She waved at some of their friends they met up with at every festival.

"Yep," she nodded, "Some of the best pickers and grinners in the biz came all the way from Mashville! It's gonna be a salt and pepper audience but we'll feel young at heart in no time when the music starts pumping through our blood!"

Twyla searched the crowd and then squealed, "The Pixie Chicks! Shadow, Mist and Light! I've just got to get their autographs!"

I'll get Fiddle a signed copy of their latest album, she decided. *Just because Fiddle didn't get to come, doesn't mean they're going to miss out completely.*

"Fiddle will love it. I know they will," said Twyla.

Twyla was glad she was allowed to go exploring on her own. Once they were unpacked, she decided to check out the vendors and get a little snack to eat. She loved walking around the carved-out acorns that housed the many different types of goodies for sale.

It kind of feels like a circus, she thought. She realized that she was drooling as she smelled the French fries, cotton candy, and fountain pollen juice. She knew she would have to pace herself because she had the whole weekend to feast on all of the delicious treats.

Don't eat too much junk food! She could hear her mother's voice in her head.

She would try some of the healthier food items like Carrot Top and Beet Green salad but there was nothing like a good old bucket of Crispy Critters. Wintergreen tea was becoming a favourite here, too. Twyla read the sign that boasted of medicinal properties in big bold letters:

INCREASED LONGEVITY!

ENHANCED MENTAL APTITUDE!

VITALITY!

"I don't know about any of that," she said to the lady behind the counter, "but I do know I would like a yummy tea, please." Maybe she would put all this healthy stuff on her list to research later.

Rubber boots and hats were the fashion of the festival.

"One must be prepared for any weather," Grandma Fannie would warn.

Sun umbrellas dotted the side hill as the crowd settled

into their favourite spots. It was strange how the sameness felt just right. Twyla was surprised she didn't find it boring, instead it was comfortable, like putting on your favourite pair of slippers. The festival had such a cozy feel. She liked listening to the chatter between each performance. It was filled with excited anticipation and favourable comments about the last band or singer.

"We're like one big happy family, eh kiddo?" said Grandpa Fog. No wonder everyone kept coming back.

The tunes, as Grandma Fannie affectionately referred to the songs, were sometimes funny with comical lyrics and a lilting beat to match; Cotton-field Joe, Sawtooth Sam, Daisy Days... the list of classics seemed endless. Then just when you were smiling from ear to ear, someone would start to sing the most mournful melody ever written. The words would string together a message of gloom and despair. Sometimes the whine of the fiddle would pluck a tear right out of your eye as everyone held their breath and prayed for the story to have a bit of a happy ending. The songs were tales of woe, heroes, hard times and each one was more endearing than the last. There were songs of shining moons and moonshine. Gleeful instrumentals sewed up the wounds that the sad song before it had left. This music was a roller coaster of life.

Twyla knew that some of her friends made fun of bluegrass because they didn't think it was as cool as pop music, but she wished that they could experience just one good old fashioned bluegrass festival and then they would understand how awesome it really was. She also wished that Fiddle was here to enjoy it with her. It was just one of the things that the two had in common and it felt odd not to share it with her cousin.

The music started early and lasted well into the evening. Some took a supper break, but even then, you could walk through the campground and hear little groups of family and friends striking up old favourites. The stage lights went off at the end of the day, and then the blistering ballads really started to resonate. Grandpa grabbed his harmonica and blew till his cheeks looked like they would explode. Twyla thought he looked like Brian Bullfrog when he tried to hit the high notes. She clapped and whistled, yelling "Go Grandpa!"

Grandma picked away on her mandolin and started to blush when others stopped to applaud. Twyla knew that Grandma Fannie had always dreamed of being a bluegrass star, but she also knew that she seemed to lack confidence in her musical abilities.

"Grandma," she asked, "why didn't you grow up to be a Bluegrass star?"

Grandma smiled. "I was too busy working back then, Twyla. Music was for dreamers and Saturday nights."

Twyla thought it was a pity that her grandma's family had not encouraged her to pursue her dreams. She clapped and cheered twice as loud, hoping that her encouragement would help her grandmother find her voice and one day sing, even if it was just for the fun of it.

Campfires and lightning bugs lit up the valley. Harmony wasn't just in the notes but in the hearts of everyone who came to listen or to play. It was a miracle of sorts to see so many different types of bugs and forest creatures forgetting their worries and just getting into the music.

Twyla wandered around looking at all the sights. Carpenter ants, flying ants and the common ones that showed up at every picnic were forming a line from one end to the other. Twyla noticed that some of them were even holding hands. She saw the Praying Mantis family heading into the chapel for gospel hour. The crickets were chirping in sync with the cicadas. The wasps and bees were hanging out over by the fence. They kept to themselves, and no one seemed to mind as long as there was enough sticky honey to go around. She smiled as she watched the moths flitting from light to light. She couldn't believe that they were in tempo with the band on stage because they seemed so disoriented.

The caterpillars were spilling out of their silky tent. The

toddler larvae were splashing in the puddles after the sun began to shine and the older bugs were soaking it up. Twyla noticed one old slug curled up in his lawn chair in the front row. She could see that his eyes were closed, and he seemed to be sleeping but yet he still fit right in. This was another mystery for Twyla to follow up on.

4

The music on stage finally stopped at the end of the night.

"Time for a power nap," announced Grandpa Fog. He promptly headed for the R.V.

Twyla and her grandmother exchanged a look between them and both had to stifle a snicker because Grandpa Fog had been sleeping in his lawn chair.

"Yes, dear," smiled Grandma Fannie. "Time to wake up and go to bed. Get a good rest, there will be plenty more good bands on tomorrow, and we want you rested up for the trip home."

He pulled her close and gave her a soft little kiss, before

he turned to Twyla.

"Now don't you keep your grandmother up all day telling stories."

Twyla flew over and gave him a kiss. She braced herself for his hug.

"Aww, come on, Grandpa Fog, just a couple..."

Twyla's fondest memories from the bluegrass festivals she went to were when her grandmother would sit with her by the fire at the end of the night.

"For the most part, I seem to have all of my solar pathway lights in a row," Grandma Fannie would say as she bent to add more wood. This made Twyla laugh.

Grandma Fannie was so full of information and she barely ever needed to use the Internet. Twyla was amazed by all the lessons she learned from her grandmother, and all of the feelings she had when Grandma was weaving one of her many stories. She twisted the thread in all the right places to make it worthwhile and funny enough, that sometimes Twyla forgot that she was learning. It was just part of the story for a bug to come away feeling like she could hold her head higher and shine brighter after a story from Grandma Fannie.

Twyla brought out two camping chairs and unfolded them. She put them right tight together so she and her grandmother would be almost as close as when they were at home cuddling on the couch. She went and got a couple of blankets in case they were chilly. She patiently watched Grandma Fannie stoking up the fire.

"Will you tell me a story, Grandma?" Twyla asked finally, when Grandma Fannie was coaxing a good flame. "Maybe one of your 'Mind the Times', the stories about when you were little."

"Now Twyla," started Grandma Fannie as she settled into the camping chair beside the fire. "You know I don't tell the usual, 'once upon a time' kind of fairy tales. My stories are about my experiences along this path toward The Land of Agelessness."

Some of Grandma Fannie's shares were short little quips about how she and her best friend Fern Flagstone used to get in trouble when they were young. Twyla found these ones cute and funny and loved when Grandma would chuckle and always start with the words:

"Mind the time Fern and I..."

The adventure would unfold and the story would end with Grandma shaking her head, slapping her knee and then wiping the joyous tears from her glasses. Sometimes when she was telling the story she seemed to forget that Twyla was listening. At these times she would catch herself, realizing that the adventures might give Twyla some ideas about trying some of the things herself.

"Don't do as I do, Twyla, Do as I say!" Grandma would say.

Hmmm, thought Twyla, *I guess even grandmothers push the boundaries sometimes!*

Twyla didn't understand every part of the stories because so much was different now compared to when her grandmother was a little bug. Sometimes she could relate easily, though, because as strange as some of it sounded, it also reminded her of the many adventures she and Fiddle got caught up in.

Grandpa Fog sometimes teased Grandma Fannie when she was telling her stories. Grandma was always quick to remind him that anyone can have a bad night or make a mistake.

"Did I ever tell you about the time that Grandpa Fog accidently tried to weld his butt?" she would say to Twyla with a wink.

Grandma Fannie embellished this story more and more each time, so Twyla could listen to this tale a million times before it would get boring. Grandpa would smile through the story too, because he loved the way Grandma told it, and he loved her imagination. In fact, he seemed to love everything about her and the way they looked at each other reminded Twyla of something soft and gooey like eating maple taffy in springtime. She thought their love for each other was sweet and sticky.

Grandma had an endless number of stories about herself. She didn't really seem to have a favourite one. Twyla didn't know what would trigger the next one or set her off to retell a newer version of an old tale. Grandma Fannie would be making supper or doing laundry and then start to chuckle and Twyla knew it was coming. From the moment Grandma wiped her hands on the apron she wore, to the last chuckle the two would have before Grandma hugged her hard and got back to the task of cooking, Twyla was wrapped up in the shawl of Grandma's love, laughter and somewhat lyrical stories of her life.

"Please tell me my favourite one, Grandma," begged Twyla, this time beside the campfire at the Ramblin' River Bluegrass Festival. "You know, the one about the swing."

Grandma Fannie cleared her throat. She sat back and took a breath before she launched into the story.

5

Fern Flagstone was my very best friend," she began. "Maybe she wasn't much for skipping stones on the lake, but she sure was solid as a rock when it came to friendship. She never got married because she gave her heart to a coal miner. Her parents did not approve of their relationship, and he moved on to the next big strike when the mine shut down. I felt sad that Fern didn't get to be with her true love, but I have to admit, I was happy that she stayed here in Bugcroft and spent her time with me."

Grandma Fannie paused and looked into the fire before she continued.

"Fern lived a good life. She was fiercely independent and loved her job at Trails End, that boutique across from the bakery in Bugcroft back in the day."

Twyla knew that Grandma Fannie missed Fern terribly since she went to the Land of Agelessness. Fern seemed like the responsible one in Grandma's 'Mind the Time' stories. Twyla was reminded suddenly of how Fern was a lot like Fiddle.

"We were about your age, I guess Twyla. We were always together, inseparable, just like you and Fiddle. One hot summer evening we went down to the pond with some of the other bugs from town. They would bring picnic baskets to cool off by the water. Some splashed around near the shore and others lined up to take turns running, leaping and falling after being suspended in air for what seemed like agelessness."

She started to chuckle with remembering.

"One time, I jumped in, and the force from the water pulled my bathing suit bottom right off! I was lucky and caught it on my toe just as it was about to sink to the bottom of the pond!" "Whew," she tried to catch her breath, laughing hard now. Sometimes Grandma would skip over that part, but this time it hit her right in the funnies.

"One really hot night, Fern and I decided to go down to the pond," Grandma Fannie's voice softened as she reminisced.

"Same as always, when we got there, Fern thought that she would just hang out on the beach with her cousins, the Pebbles. I couldn't help myself, and dared her to try the old swing. I was so excited that she was finally going to join in the fun! She stood in line in front of me and the sweat dripped off her. I'm not sure if it was from the heat of the summer or from being nervous."

Fern knew she would never have considered giving this a try if Fannie hadn't dared her. Her mother had told her that it was not really an appropriate activity for someone in the Flagstone family. Fern never challenged her mother's wisdom, but Fannie had gone on and on about her being afraid of a bit of water.

"Quit crowding me," she said to Fannie. "What's the big hurry?"

"You're up!" Fannie squealed with glee and ran toward her friend.

Fern thought that Fannie was going to push her in, so she leapt with all of her strength toward the swing. It groaned a bit with her weight, but as she held on, it swung out over the deepest part of the pond. With her eyes tightly shut she screamed and let go.

"Whee!" she screamed.

The ride down was exhilarating but didn't last very long.

Thud!

She hit the bottom, sinking into the thick mud, and she knew right away that she should have heeded her mother's warnings.

"This is not for me," she realized, watching the bubbles go up from her lips to the surface far above. Thick mud pulled around her and with a heavy sigh she realized that her fate was up to her friends.

Meanwhile, on the shore, Fannie felt a bit sorry that she had taken this opportunity to have a laugh at Fern's expense. She loved her friend dearly, and yet again found that her practical joke went a bit too far. She ran down the shore and found Roger Raccoon digging clams for his lunch.

"Please Roger," she pleaded, "come and dig Fern out! She's stuck on the bottom and it's all my fault!"

He waddled down the beach and flicked Fern out with ease. Everyone clapped when Fern popped out spluttering. She was frowning, but after a moment she grinned. She wouldn't be doing that again, but she was proud to do it once and for all.

"That was one of the best days in my life," smiled Grandma Fannie. "There have been lots of good times and Fern was right there beside me through most of them. She was as excited as I was the time we went to the city and saw Molly Reardon, our favourite country singer on stage. It was risky but well worth the trip."

Remembering Fern was bittersweet. It made Grandma Fannie happy when she remembered the good times they had together, but it made her sad when she thought about how much she missed her friend. Fern had been taken to the city in a big dump truck and even though Fannie didn't really know her fate, she knew she would never see her again.

Grandma Fannie glanced at her watch.

"Oh my, it's way too late to start into the story of Molly Reardon. It's a long one and I don't want to give you any ideas about straying too far away from Bugcroft... maybe when you're a bit older."

Twyla had overheard this story many times when she was listening from the bedroom when Grandma Fannie thought she was asleep. Twyla was glad that her grandmother was brave enough to have such amazing experiences with her friend when she was younger and couldn't wait until she and Fiddle could go exploring again.

Twyla could hardly wrap her buzzing head around the thought of elders playing as children, but to top it off, as her grandmother was tucking her into bed, she got very solemn, almost like when she sat in contemplation and started to talk about the Land of Agelessness. This was a topic that was even harder for Twyla to understand. According to her grandmother, this great mystery was glorious. Time was not only ageless but endless there. Grandma Fannie explained that even though she had not been there, she knew deep down in her soul that it was as real as the shimmer in Twyla's butt.

"It's a place where everyone goes eventually," said Grandma Fannie, "but no one knows when or why their travels will take them there. It is a beautiful place where there is no worry or stress... where no one gets sick and where everyone is treated equally. It's a place where no one would even consider telling tall tales about each other... where sadness is fleeting, and peace abounds."

Twyla could tell by the look in Grandma's eyes that this was one story she not only believed but even if she added to it, it would still all be true. It was a place of miracles and even when described by her grandmother, who was the most incredible storyteller, it was indescribable.

Twyla would love to believe that the Land of Agelessness was true. It was not just Grandma Fannie's stories; many talked of it. She had not seen it for herself, nor did she know anyone who had seen this treasured land with their own eyes. How could somewhere like this be so accepted to be truth and yet so elusive? How come no one ever got to see it? The other questions that Twyla pondered and researched to her heart's content seemed so small in comparison to the questions surrounding the Land of Agelessness. Where was it?

Twyla was perplexed. She knew that the thought of the Land of Agelessness gave a sense of peace to others that had relatives and friends travel to this land and pass into its beauty. She had been told of its existence before she could even tie her little fly shoes, so the story was stuck in her mind.

If only I could go there and collect some proof, she thought. *Even meteorites leave a bit of a clue behind. Maybe this will be my lifelong quest. Maybe I will be able to find out so that I can help others find the peace the Land of Agelessness brings, and even find it for myself.*

She drifted off to sleep trying to imagine what it might look like there.

6

The moon came streaming in through the window and Twyla knew it was time to get up. She stretched and smiled as she reflected on her weekend. She was sad that the festival was over already, and that they would be heading home soon. She liked the safe feeling she had laying here but she knew it was time to get looking for Fiddle. She couldn't believe that her cousin was still not answering her texts or emails. Where could Fiddle possibly be?

She closed her eyes and whispered, "Wherever are you, Fiddle?" Then she added, "Don't worry, I'll find you."

She choked back a tear as she realized that for the first time, she was thinking the worst. "I'm so scared that Fiddle has gone to The Land of Agelessness," she admitted.

Twyla knew that more and more bugs were going there as the city of Peopleborough got bigger and bigger. She remembered Grandma's warnings about going too far past the Bugcroft limits.

"Twyla, you stay close to home now," Grandma Fannie would caution. "Those city dwellers are encroaching on our land and it just isn't safe for a little bug to go too far."

Twyla shook her head hard to make the negative thoughts stop. She knew that Fiddle was not as curious as she was, and hoped with all of her heart that Fiddle was not in the 'wrong place at the wrong time'. That's what Grandpa Fog said had happened to too many bugs.

"Not Fiddle!" she yelled as she jumped out of bed.

Twyla slept through the ride home from the festival. She was glad that she could start looking for Fiddle. She rushed through breakfast, only picking at her food because she was not very hungry. She knew that Grandma Fannie would never let her go off without at least attempting to eat a little bit.

"I really have to get going and find Fiddle," she said. She jumped off her stool as soon as she was finished, and flew to give her grandma a kiss before she headed out for the night. She buzzed by Grandpa Fog's chair and braced herself for one of his bear hugs.

"Love you lots, Twyla," they both called.

"See you soon! 'Cause I love you both, too."

Twyla hoped she would find Fiddle quickly tonight so that they could come by and have some of Grandma Fannie's yummy treats and listen to some bluegrass together. She couldn't wait to give Fiddle the new albums she bought them and catch up on all they had missed.

Twyla started asking everywhere and everyone if they had seen Fiddle. Mysteriously, no one had. Although Fiddle had other interests and lots of things to occupy their time, two weeks was a long time for Fiddle not to have any contact with Twyla, or not to have at least been noticed around Bugcroft. Twyla was not a fan of gossip, but the good side to it was that in a small town, usually someone had an idea of where you were, and more than likely, a detailed account of what you were doing. Not always reliable, gossip was a form of entertainment to some. Twyla's questions about Fiddle's whereabouts had started the ol' gossip mill churning, and Twyla was not feeling very positive about finding Fiddle.

How can no one have seen anything? she wondered.

Missing Fiddle felt horrible. Twyla knew that her sadness was partly responsible for feeling so tired. Her cousin was not just a relative, but they had become such good friends over their whole lives together. Fiddle came along with Twyla on adventures, and provided the accompaniment when Twyla was secretly practicing the song she wrote for her grandparents. Their anniversary was soon, and they needed to practice until the whole piece fit together like a hand in a glove. Twyla wrote the sentimental lyrics that would ensure there would not be a dry eye in the house, and Fiddle helped her compose a two-part harmony that would touch each and every soul that ever had the pleasure of knowing the pair of love-bugs.

Twyla had to get going!

"Get your pins in under you." She could hear her Grandma Fannie encouraging her in her mind.

I have to find Fiddle soon or we won't have time to practice the song for the party.

She buckled down and started asking herself the questions she needed in order to get busy.

"Where will I start?"

"Who will I ask for help?"

Then she started to hear that old familiar hum. She looked back over her shoulder and with the power of a superhero she shouted:

"Here I glow again!"

Twyla had an idea. She zipped over to the local newspaper office to talk to Stewart Rabbit.

Stewart, Stew as he was known by friends, seemed like an older, more tired version of the Mad Hatter from Alice in Wonderland. His belly hung over his waistcoat from way too many doughnut holes and not nearly enough carrots. When his bifocals slipped down on his nose it always made Twyla feel like he was literally looking down on her. He had an air of superiority about him because of the ease with which he was able to turn from brown to white and back again with the changing of the seasons. He seemed to plod along instead of hop about and he always seemed preoccupied. The rumours about him ran rampant. Some folks said that it was time he retired, and others said that he had the ability to write bestsellers if he could just stay focused on one topic long enough.

"I am going to need posters and front-page coverage to

get this Amber Alert under way!" said Twyla with gusto.

Stewart Rabbit looked down at her with his usual unimpressed expression.

"Oh Stew, my cousin Fiddle has been missing for two weeks!" cried Twyla. She choked back her tears as she explained why she was there. "It's just not like Fiddle to not check in with me, we have never gone this long without talking! Even when one of us was away on vacation." She hung her head. "It's really not like Fiddle and I am getting very worried."

Stew knew that the fireflies were well known for their adventures, but he also knew that you never saw one of them without the other very often, and he sensed that Twyla was not exaggerating. Like any good reporter, his interest was piqued. He raised one grey eyebrow.

"Stop the presses... Today's headline will be: 'FIDDLE IS MISSING!'"

The bugs in the midst of preparing the news sighed with frustration but adjusted to run the new headline.

He took the only photo of Fiddle that Twyla had, and peered at it with a frown as he ran off several copies on his copy machine. He wrote "LOST" in big bold letters.

"I will run the story today in the Bugcroft Times," he said, as he handed her a stack of the missing posters. Twyla knew that she could count on Stew to run a headline story in the daily paper that would catch the attention of everyone in the area and those subscribing for kilometres around.

"Thank you, Stew, I knew I could count on you." Twyla felt better already just knowing that she had some help. "We'll find Fiddle. I know we will!"

As Twyla headed out the door to post the notices Stew made, she was nearly run over by someone rushing in.

"Uncle Wesley, she cried, I am so glad you're here!"

"I came as soon as I heard," he said. He grabbed her and hugged her until she was gasping a bit for air.

Uncle Wesley was known for being courageous because he lived in Peopleborough and had more street sense than the other flies in town. He was her dad's brother, but the two were as different as mud pies and cherry cheesecake. Uncle Wesley was generous and brought her family thoughtful little presents when he came to spend the weekend. He played his guitar for Grandma Fannie and you couldn't even tell from his expression that he knew every request she was going to make and exactly in which order. Twyla was sure that if that whole runs-in-the-family thing that Grandpa talked about was true, then she got her musical talent from both Grandma Fannie and Uncle Wesley. Her other uncle, Fiddle's dad, "couldn't carry a tune in a basket" but he was really good at drawing, and she loved to watch him sketch flowers in the meadow. Uncle Wesley got her a sketchbook and encouraged her to explore all areas of creativity.

With the extra help, they were able to plaster the town with missing posters in no time. Twyla even had time to stop in to have a quick chat with Brian Bullfrog, the lawyer and private investigator in town. He couldn't make ends meet with just one practice, but between the search for justice for some of his clients and the search for truth for others he kept busy. Twyla liked Brian all right but kept her hand on the doorknob as they discussed Fiddle's disappearance. She was willing to look past his warts but there was nothing wrong with being cautious. He dressed sharp and talked like a politician and that tongue could come barreling a bug's way with little to no warning and then someone else would be reporting her missing!

"S-s-so", Brian," Twyla stuttered, "If you hear or see anything about Fiddle you will let me know right away, right?"

He stared at her with his big wet eyes.

"You are the best detective I know. Please help us get Fiddle home safely," she pleaded, hoping that his heart was bigger than his stomach. She hoped that by complimenting him she could keep him from thinking about eating Fiddle.

The whole town was a-buzz with the news about Fiddle, and Twyla took comfort in the action they were taking. Now that everyone was aware that Fiddle was missing, Twyla was hopeful that Fiddle would be found soon.

Safe and sound, that's all Twyla could wish for.

She tried not to let her mind wander into negative territory. She must keep thinking positive, keep up her spirits and stay strong for Fiddle's sake. She imagined that her cousin was just gone on an adventure of their own and was counting daisy petals in a nearby field at this very moment. Maybe their phone is broken or maybe they're just too busy to come by.

Twyla couldn't let her imagination get the better of her or the tears that were very close to the surface would start to fall. She stayed focused on the search and decided she would worry about her own feelings later. She squeezed her eyes shut.

"In no time we'll be together again... soon..." she whispered. "Please, Fiddle. Please come back safe. I miss you so much it hurts."

7

"Not one leaf unturned, and not one community member not on the lookout, and still no sign of Fiddle!" Twyla cried.

She was losing hope and feeling exhausted because the long search had not turned up any clues. She spent most of her time in the makeshift command headquarters that they had set up in Grandpa Fog's garage. She stared at the map of the area over and over, hoping to see something that she had missed in previous attempts. She studied the marks representing the areas already covered and the porcupine quill pins that they used to plan the searches.

"Nothing!" she cried. "It seems like Fiddle has just vanished into thin air!"

Twyla tried thinking like her cousin to come up with

ideas on where Fiddle might be. She strained her little brain so hard she gave herself a headache. Grandma Fannie told her it was just stress related and gave her a cup of wintergreen tea to help her feel better. As Twyla sipped the tea and gazed at the map, she realized that there was one area that was not on the map.

Just off to the northeast corner of the forest was the forbidden area where bugs never ventured. Twyla had overlooked it until right now at this very moment.

"The Family Farm," she gasped. "How could I have missed it?"

Is it possible that Fiddle went that far away? she thought. Twyla couldn't imagine Fiddle going there but where else could they be?

Twyla jumped up from the toadstool she was sitting on and nearly bumped into the thistle security system that Grandpa Fog used to keep intruders out. Twyla thought it was funny to be so worried about someone trying to break into his garage. It was full of rusty old parts and tools that others had thrown away.

"One bug's rags were another bug's riches," he would say.

Twyla did not really understand what he meant by

this, although there was also a huge pile of old rags in the cupboard in the corner. Twyla shook her head, trying to focus on the task at hand. She would ask Grandpa Fog about it later because right now she had a bad feeling that Fiddle might have wandered too close to Boundary Road! It wasn't really in their nature, but since Twyla was almost out of options, she was going to round up a search party and head to the Family Farm.

Twyla avoided Grandma Fannie the whole rest of the night because she knew that she would try to talk her out of going so close to danger. The area was out of bounds because of the many stories told by some who had gone there and returned to tell of the horrors they had seen. It was like the Land of Agelessness in some respects because most never returned. The stories were scary, and Twyla was not convinced that they weren't true even though she usually challenged everything.

She remembered the story about Stew Rabbit going there to get a scoop for his paper. She recalled that it was when he was much younger and able to hop fast or he might not have been able to escape. He went late at night to check out the newly plowed plot of land that the Family was digging to expand their organic garden. The rumours about the garden being almost as big as the quarry were hard to believe and Stew felt it was his job to set the record straight.

Stew was surprised to find not only the garden, but several greenhouses full of wonderful plants just bursting with flavour. How could a rabbit resist having just a nibble of parsley or a taste of thyme before he went back to his boring life of clover and dandelions in the meadow? Stew was fast asleep in the corner of the greenhouse when the sun came up. Even though he was sleeping, he had a grin on his face as he dreamt of new varieties of organic carrots in all the colours of the rainbow.

Stew awoke in fright when he heard the roar of the tractor just after daylight. He also heard the laughter and squeals of delight as the children of the Family went running down the lane to catch the school bus. His heart pumped hard and he decided to make a run for it. He raced past the partially assembled scarecrow with the menacing face and scurried under the protection of the trees at the edge of the Forest. He did not stop running until he was safe in his warren and even then, he stayed hidden under his bed until his panic subsided.

"Oh yes," Stew recounted, "I lived to tell the tale of being on the other side of Boundary Road, but I got lucky, and I would never go again."

Twyla knew that it would be difficult, if not impossible, to get anyone to go with her to explore this area.

I will just have to go by myself, she realized. *This way there will be less chance of anyone trying to talk me out of my plan, or worse… trying to stop me.*

Gathering all of the necessary equipment she needed in one pile, Twyla packed her backpack with an extra jug of clean water and some dried wintergreen berries, along with her maps and compass. A survival and remedy pack all in one.

Who knows what I will come across? she thought. *When I find Fiddle, I have to be prepared for the worst…*

She packed her tiny sleeping bag in case she had to stay longer than expected. She knew that Grandma Fannie would be frantic with worry, so she made up a story about going to stay with Uncle Wesley in the city. She would text her mom and dad when she was across Boundary Road. They would be upset because she did not have their permission, but it was not nearly as bad as them knowing that she was going to the Family Farm.

I might get grounded forever! she thought.

She hoped that she would be back from her search, with Fiddle by her side, before any further fibs or explanations were needed.

I know they'll all understand, she tried to reassure herself. *I just hope this all works out okay. I know Fiddle would do the same for me. I really don't have any choice.*

Twyla felt as prepared as she ever would. She hiked her bulging backpack over her shoulder and took one long last look in the mirror of her dresser. She looked deep into her own eyes trying to find a glimpse of the superhero she often pretended to be when no one was looking. She gave herself a courage pep talk and reminded herself that the risk was well worth getting her beloved cousin back where they belonged. She did not even question what she would do if she couldn't find Fiddle. This was the last resort, and Fiddle just had to be there.

8

Hidden in between two dried out pine cones at the edge of the Forest, Twyla rested and contemplated her plan of attack. She was very glad that the longest part of the trip was over. She could see the Family Farm just across the field from her hiding spot. She knew that there were many dangers on the Farm and the ones that she was aware of were probably less dangerous than the ones that she didn't even know about yet. She took a few minutes to research farm dangers before she packed for her trip and the list seemed so daunting, she just scanned it quickly. Farm equipment, implements, pesticides, animals. There was even a picture of a pitchfork! It said that it was used to move things around like hay and manure, but it sure looked like it could do a lot of damage to a tiny firefly. The only good thing about being so little would be that she might fit between the tines if the sharp points missed her. Eeeek!

This list of problems did not even include the Family Members. They were giants. Sure, she thought, the children seemed a bit less frightening when she saw them playing in the yard on their jumping machine, but their feet could destroy several fireflies at once just by accident. They did not even have to be bullies. Twyla would need to be very cautious and choose her timing carefully.

She watched and waited. The smaller giants had finished jumping on their jumping machine and gone inside. The tractor was shut down. All the Family Members seemed to be inside their house. Twyla decided that it must be their supper time, so everyone would be in one place. She took a sip of water and pretended it was as full of courage as it was of refreshment.

"It's now or never!" she told herself.

Off she flew from the protection of the Forest's edge to the windowsill of the Farmhouse.

"Whew!" she whispered.

That was a record-breaking time for her. It was surprising how fast she could go when she was in danger. Just making it this far grew her confidence. She peered in the window with as little movement as possible, and was grateful that it was still daylight so that she was not lighting up and alerting anyone to her presence.

What she saw was scarier than any scene she had ever witnessed in her bug life.

The Family Members were all seated at the table eating and sharing stories. Their giant mouths were chewing and talking so loud that she could hear the sound through the window. They were enormous and just looking at them all together was overwhelming. The dad was the largest of them all but even the baby in her booster chair was intimidating to Twyla.

As she watched, she got used to the scene and her nerves calmed down. She noticed that the Family was laughing and sharing in much the same way as her family did when they got together for a meal. She also noticed that they all had a bit of a glow around them. It was not like the firefly glow; it was kind of blurry and not as bright. Somehow Twyla knew instantly that it was love. She didn't know how she knew and she certainly had not come across this in her research. She assumed that Grandma must have talked about this in one of her many wise stories.

Twyla relaxed a bit knowing that the Family was full

of love. It gave her hope that they would not harm Fiddle intentionally and as long as she stayed away from their ginormous feet, she might be safe as well.

When the meal was over the children of the Family grabbed one of the almost empty water glasses and a few crumbs and went straight to the corner of the room. Twyla was starting to feel the glowing sensation in her butt as she wondered where they were going and what they were up to. The dad stayed at the table with the baby as the two older children went to the corner of the room.

"What the heck?" Twyla wondered. The corner seemed to be some sort of sanctuary. There was a glass box with brightly coloured fish in it. One of the children put sprinkles of some kind on the top and the fish swam up to get it.

They are feeding the fish, Twyla realized.

Twyla was surprised at the joy in the eyes of all of the Family Members as they watched the fish eating. Then the older child picked up a jar that had mesh covering the top and held it as gently as if it were a dried maple leaf. The children touched the jar, and their auras glowed brighter.

Suddenly Twyla gasped. To her astonishment, her cousin, Fiddle, was nestled in a soft pile of milkweed feathers inside the jar.

Twyla wanted to yell "Fiddle! Fiddle! I'm here!" but she remained very still and continued to watch closely. Her cousin did not look frightened. Fiddle looked sick and seemed to be soothed by the comforting words of the older child. If Twyla had not seen this with her own eyes, she would believe none of it. She rubbed her eyes several times to make sure she was seeing correctly and not hallucinating from her long flight.

No, it was real, she thought. *Even Grandma Fannie couldn't have imagined anything like this.*

Twyla was relieved that she had found her cousin and instead of fearing for Fiddle's life, was instantly glad that the Family were taking care of them.

I wonder what happened to Fiddle, she thought as she tried to keep from lighting up. She could barely contain herself on the window ledge. She wanted to throw all caution to the wind and go barging in there, but she wasn't sure it was the right thing to do. She had been taught to fear the Family, and this fear ran deep. She felt like this might be an outdated way of thinking but did not want to jeopardize her mission to rescue Fiddle by acting too quickly. Grandma Fannie had pointed out in the past that Twyla was too trusting when she got herself into trouble, so she decided that this time she would just bide her time and be patient.

"If you're ever in a knot, patience can untie it. Patience can do many things. Have you ever tried it?"

Oh, it was as if Grandma Fannie was right here with her.

She was so glad that all of the important lessons seemed to pop up right when she needed them.

Twyla pulled out her sleeping bag and took up her stake-out position with renewed energy. It might be a long wait, but she felt confident that Fiddle was being well cared for, and when her cousin was healthy again, Twyla would be right here waiting for them and they would be on their way home.

9

Twyla woke with a start.

She could not believe that she fell asleep. Here she was, on active guard duty, her cousin's life depending on her, and she nodded off. Even worse, she woke up to find six giant sparkling eyes staring at her from inside the window. The older children and the baby were standing there with their noses pressed right up against the window. The baby's nose was cute like a little button, but kind of gross and slimy and looked like it needed a good wipe! It left little marks on the window, and as usual Twyla was distracted by her curiosity for details, but she shook her head to focus on the disaster at hand: she was busted.

Oh no, she thought, *I must have been having inquisitive dreams! I must have been glowing all night long and the Family was able to spot me easily.*

Her mind raced with questions.

How could I let this happen?

How could I let Fiddle down?

What will I do now?

Her reeling mind stuttered to a halt as she caught the expressions of the children staring at her. They were smiling at her kindly.

There is that strange glow again! she thought.

Could they be looking at her with love? Was it possible that all the gossip about them was wrong and they really meant her and Fiddle no harm?

Twyla could only hope that was the case, because if the pudgy little one turned on them, they would be nothing but a smear, much like the nose press that she left on the window!

There was an older human speaking to the children. Twyla decided that she must be their grandmother. Her voice was soothing, and reminded Twyla of the tone her own grandmother used when she was talking to her grandchildren, or when she was reminding them to do something important. Twyla was really starting to believe that this Family was as nice as her own. Just because they were bigger and different didn't mean that they were unkind. Everything she knew before from second-hand knowledge seemed rather silly as she stood face-to-face with them. She saw them doing kind acts for each other, for the fish, and especially for Fiddle. She saw the glowing love they shared when they gave the Family Dog a pat on the head or snuck him a scrap under the table. It was in her very nature to question their behaviours because of the stories that she had heard, but the proof was right here in front of her. She took a chance and smiled back, her butt glowing bright.

The children clapped excitedly, and Twyla almost lost her balance at the vibrations. She steadied herself on the windowsill and realized that they understood she was there for Fiddle and her presence made them all very happy. They ran to get the jar that held Fiddle, and as soon as they put it up to the window, Twyla could see Fiddle raise their head. Fiddle was weak but they smiled and gave Twyla a reassuring wink. The children ran to the grandmother human and Twyla could see her nodding her head. She reached down and gave the jar a pat as if it was a child of her own, and Fiddle started to get their glow back a bit.

Human love is powerful, Twyla thought. She could feel it right through the window and she knew that there was nothing to fear.

The older children came running outside. The child with the jar tried to be careful not to jolt Fiddle too much. They came right up to the window. The Baby watched from inside.

The human child opened the jar and gently slid Fiddle out to land softly beside Twyla. Twyla didn't realize that she was holding her breath until Fiddle reached out and hugged her, popping the last little bit of air out of her.

They had tears in their eyes as they looked each other over in disbelief. When they realized that they were both okay, they started to giggle.

"So where have you been?" Twyla said.

"Hanging out with my new friends," said Fiddle with a weak grin. They hugged each other tight again.

"I guess it will be a while before we top this one!" Fiddle added.

They were so intent on each other and being reunited that they didn't even notice the children had gone back into the kitchen. They were smiling from the window but had tears in their eyes too. There was something else there too. Twyla saw pride in the grandmother's glow, and much like love it seemed to have a radiance of its own. The Family sat back down at the table for breakfast, and although Twyla couldn't make out their chatter, she had a feeling they were talking about what happened as if it had been a big adventure for them too.

"Oh Fiddle, I was so worried about you," said Twyla. "I missed you more than you will ever know."

She didn't admit to her cousin that she was afraid that they had gone to the Land of Agelessness. Those thoughts all seemed silly now that she knew Fiddle was here all along.

"Why on earth would you go to the Family Farm? You know how dangerous it is...er... how dangerous it's supposed to be."

Twyla was confused about finding out that everything she once believed had changed. She was also a bit dazed from sleeping at night and being awake in the morning. Everything was upside down.

Fiddle was still a bit shaky.

"Tell me what happened," said Twyla.

Fiddle recounted the tale.

Fiddle had accidentally swallowed some dew drops that were full of pesticides. Normally fireflies loved dewdrops, but these were toxic to fireflies and most other living creatures. The Family could tell that Fiddle was in trouble and took them home to take care of them. Fiddle might have died if the giant children had not nursed them back to health.

Twyla gulped and choked back a tear as she realized that Fiddle might have really ended up in the Land of Agelessness instead of just in a jar at the Family Farm.

"Wow, Fiddle," remarked Twyla. "I'm so glad that the Family turned out to be so loving, and I am glad that you are going to be okay."

After a refreshing snack of wintergreen berries to boost their energy and a couple of Caramel Critters, the bugs washed down the treat with some fresh dew drops that Twyla had stored in her backpack and soon they were eager to leave.

The cousins turned and waved through the window as the Family watched their little bug friends take flight. They both laughed out loud when the baby blew them a kiss. They quickly blew one back and they were on their way home.

10

'TWYLA RESCUES FIDDLE' blasted the headline the next day in the Bugcroft Times.

Stew Rabbit made a point of interviewing the two himself in order to get the facts right.

Stew asked Fiddle to tell their story and although they were usually quite shy and didn't like all of the attention like Tywla did, Fiddle recounted what they could remember.

"I was just going to check out the big tree down by the creek to see if Dad was there painting a landscape, and I got curious and kept going," said Fiddle.

"How very like a firefly," said Stew Rabbit. "Go on."

"I guess I wandered a bit too far. I only wanted to say goodbye and get a hug before I went with Twyla to the Ramblin' River Bluegrass Festival. I was so excited to go again this year! I know we're not supposed to drink dewdrops if we don't know if they're safe, but I was really thirsty and took a chance," recalled Fiddle.

"The next thing I knew, I started feeling really sick. I got dizzy and just before I passed out, I saw the Family! I was scared but there wasn't a thing I could do."

Fiddle turned to their cousin.

"Twyla, I was wishing so hard that you were there with me to help and then everything went dark. I don't know how long I slept... in fact I don't remember much of anything until just a couple of days ago when I woke up and realized that I was at the Family Farm!"

Fiddle took a deep breath and then continued. "I was still feeling pretty yucky when I woke up, and I was worried that I wouldn't get to see any of my family again... especially you, Twyla, my best friend."

Twyla smiled, and stayed quiet for once, wrapped up in the story.

"Sure, sometimes you push the limits and get us in trouble but we also do lots of things together that don't get us into trouble."

Twyla had to laugh at that. "Like the time we organized the fundraiser to help injured firefly larvae," chimed in Twyla.

"Yes," agreed Fiddle, "or the time we stayed up all day and night and day again just to see if we could! Nope, we aren't always getting into trouble."

Twyla knew that Fiddle loved listening to music and enjoyed going to the Ramblin' River Bluegrass Festival, but their heart's desire was to help others; especially bugs who didn't feel that they fit in. They knew they could always talk to Fiddle about their fears and worries without feeling like they were being judged or made fun of. Fiddle was the one that made everyone feel at home even when their home didn't feel safe or when they didn't quite know who they wanted to be.

Twyla called Fiddle a 'trailblazer' which sounded like someone out in the forest building a path but really meant that just by being their own true self, Fiddle inspired others to do the same.

"It didn't take me long to figure out that the Family were taking care of me. It kind of blew my mind. I thought that they were supposed to be mean, but they helped me," Fiddle explained to Stew.

The rabbit nodded in agreement, encouraging Fiddle to go on with their story.

"It was really weird being awake in the daytime and asleep at night, but I really liked watching the Family and learning about them. I was so surprised that I could see their love glowing. It felt perfectly normal, like I was right at home. They didn't seem to care how I looked or what

I wore, they just cared that I was getting better. It was amazing to be treated like one of them even though we are very different creatures. Without the Family taking care of me I don't know what would have happened."

Stew thought back to his experience at the Farm. Fiddle's experience was quite different.

What a great twist on the story, he thought. *The twist of the century!*

He ended the interview.

"Well, folks, you heard it here first! Fiddle, we are so glad that Twyla found you and brought you back home. You two are the bravest little fireflies in Bugcroft! I thought I had seen and heard it all!" He couldn't wait to get the story out.

The whole town was talking about the big rescue. Twyla was having a hard time letting it all sink in.

"I always knew you were the smartest and bravest little bug in Bugcroft!" said Grandma Fannie. Then she checked her all over to make sure that she really was okay.

"Oh, Grandma Fannie, I was never in any real danger," blushed Twyla.

She didn't know how a hero was supposed to feel and

all of the attention was making her a bit uncomfortable. She hoped that everyone would forget about the whole ordeal and get back to normal.

Twyla's family was a bit upset with her for going on the rescue mission by herself, but she could tell that they were very proud of her for being a hero too. Still, she was grounded for her reckless behaviour for her own good, at least for a while. She had to stay with her grandparents for punishment. She got to eat her favourite snacks and curl up close to Grandma Fannie while Grandpa Fog reread the newspaper article that had made Twyla famous. She enjoyed the safe feeling of being surrounded by loved ones.

Twyla was anxious about being separated from Fiddle again, both because she missed her cousin, and because they really needed to get working on the anniversary party planning for Grandma Fannie and Grandpa Fog.

Finally, Twyla convinced her grandparents to let her go out and see Fiddle. Grandma Fannie remembered how she missed Fern.

Twyla and Fiddle convinced Uncle Wesley to help them practice their special song. They spent their nights preparing for the party, and now the time the cousins spent together had more meaning than ever because of Fiddle's brush with the Land of Agelessness. They hugged each other every few minutes.

Bugs were taught that the Family was more destructive than respectful. Stories about how the humans' ancestors had scarred the face of the earth were told at bug gatherings. Twyla made a mental note to start attending the Town Hall meetings so that she could set the record straight. It was important to her that folks understood that the Family must have changed their destructive way of living over the past couple of generations and indeed were devoting their time and energy to better things, like organic farming without pesticides.

Uncle Wesley enjoyed listening to Fiddle's story too. He told them that he believed that things were really changing for the good.

"The folks in Peopleborough are starting to build what they call Green Zones right in the heart of the city. It's nice for bugs like me to have a safe place to gather and jam with my friends."

"Oh my goodness!!" exclaimed Fiddle.

"What?"

"In all the excitement I forgot to tell you the best part of the adventure!"

"Well what is it?!" said Twyla.

"I met the one and only Molly Reardon!"

Molly Reardon was Grandma Fannie and her best friend Fern's favourite musician, the one they saw in concert on the best adventure of their lives.

"How?" asked Twyla.

"She's the grandmother to the children of the Family, she grew up at the Family Farm. She stopped in for a visit. I was front row and center to a private concert right there in the kitchen of the Family Farm."

"I can't believe it!" Twyla squealed. Grandma Fannie had a postage stamp poster of Molly Reardon hanging on the wall. It showed off the big blond puff of hair that framed Molly's smiling face, and her sparkling jewels. Grandma explained that she had 'the voice of an angel' and she daydreamed of meeting Molly for real. Sometimes she would wink and say, "it's a good thing she isn't a bug, or your grandpa would be worried I would run away with her!"

Twyla's thoughts tumbled in overtime, and she had a brilliant idea.

"What if you asked Molly Reardon to perform at the

anniversary party?"

A human performer would shock the bugs, but it would be a dream come true for her grandma and grandpa.

"Do you think she would?" asked Fiddle skeptically.

"Why not?" Twyla was already searching for Molly's website and getting ready for Fiddle to write the star a message.

Dear Molly,

You may not remember me, but I am the little bug your grandchildren kept in the jar, beside the fish. I am so grateful that they nursed me back to health when I was very, very sick. My cousin Twyla came to rescue me, but she would have been too late if your grandchildren hadn't found me. Twyla's Grandma Fannie and Grandpa Fog are in love with you! Never in a million years would they believe they would get to meet you!

I know you are a very busy
person, being the best bluegrass
singer ever, but we are planning
a surprise anniversary party
for them, and we wish with all
our hearts, my best friend Twyla
and I, if you could come and
sing for them. It would mean
the world to me to pull off such
a surprise and bring them that
much joy!

I have included the party
details here, and also the song
we have written for them.
Please, oh please, come and help
Twyla and I to sing it strong!

Love,

Fiddle and Twyla Firefly

"Does this sound good?" asked Fiddle.

"It looks great! Don't send it yet..." Twyla attached the lyrics that had been going round and round in her head ever since she started thinking about the party and crossed her fingers and toes before she hit send.

Invitations were sent to everyone, and Stewart Rabbit even agreed to run an advertisement in the paper so no one was left out. The trick that Twyla came up with to keep the anniversary part a secret was brilliant. She was advertising it as Fiddle's Welcome Home Party so that Grandma Fannie and Grandpa Fog would be surprised when they realized that the party was actually in their honour. It was such a good plan, right down to the last decoration.

Twyla kept checking her inbox, hoping that Molly Reardon would see their message and respond.

The party theme was Fireworks. This was because Grandma Fannie said that she knew Grandpa Fog was the one because she saw fireworks with her eyes closed the first time Grandpa kissed her way back in the day.

Twyla stuck sparklers around the stage. She and Fiddle got the local baker to make the most amazing cake. It displayed two hearts linked together, and one had the face of Grandpa Fog looking towards the other one that had the smiling face of Grandma Fannie with her beautiful eyes twinkling. Twyla wasn't sure how they had pulled it off so beautifully, with special icing and everything. There was a "Snail and Slug" buffet, and all of their other favourite treats.

What a feast! What a party!

Twyla wanted everything to be so perfect for Grandma Fannie and Grandpa Fog, and Fiddle wanted it to be perfect for Twyla.

Twyla was disappointed that Molly Reardon had not responded, but the party would be spectacular no matter what. She decided that she had better get together with Fiddle and practice the special song one more time. She knew that Uncle Wesley would back them up on guitar and his sweet licks would hide any imperfections in their bug voices.

No deceiving, never leaving…

This is love…

Twyla cooed through the chorus as Fiddle harmonized softly with her.

Stay together, for forever…

This is love.

They were snuggled in bed practicing until their eyes were heavy with sleep, feeling very confident that all of their hard work and planning would come together perfectly at the party. Before falling asleep, Twyla put in one more little wish on a prayer that Molly Reardon would show up to sing, and then sleep came quickly.

11

The music was loud, and the stage was lit up like a Christmas tree. It was remarkable that Squirrel Haggard and Nellie Wilson showed up to play with Patsy Vine. Grandma Fannie and Grandpa Fog had met some amazing musicians in their time, and they were well-appreciated fans. The amazing musicians played songs that Grandma Fannie referred to as 'oldies but goodies'. Grandma Fannie swooned when Squirrel started singing 'Old Flames Can't Hold a Candle to You'. Twyla saw Grandpa Fog pull her a little tighter.

"This used to be our theme song," he said softly. They swayed to the music still in disbelief that Twyla had surprised them with such an amazing party for their anniversary.

In the breaks when the band was having a rest, Twyla played a list of songs that she had chosen just for the occasion. 'You Light Up My Life' and 'Light My Fire' might just be her new favourites. They were not bluegrass but sure had a nice ring to them. She also loved 'This Little Light of Mine', and 'I Saw the Light' had everyone up out of their seats. There was lots of clapping and toe tapping to each one as it blared over the speakers.

Twyla and Fiddle were both anxious and excited to step out onto the stage. It was time for their big number. With Uncle Wesley accompanying them, they began to sing.

Grandma Fannie and Grandpa Fog had tears of happiness in their eyes listening to Twyla and Fiddle's sweet little voices.

Suddenly the place went still. The long grass behind the stage parted to reveal kind eyes and a large puff of blond hair dotted with rhinestones.

It was Molly Reardon! She joined in just in time for the chorus.

No deceiving, never leaving…

This is love…

Twyla's mouth dropped open and she whirled around to see the Queen of Country Music & Conservation all rolled into one.

"Molly, you came!" she shouted. She was ecstatic that Molly had answered her email or prayer or however she had gotten here. Twyla and Fiddle pulled themselves together to finish the song. They grabbed hands and sang their hearts out.

When the audience finally stopped cheering, in her signature style, Molly started to rhyme. She looked directly at Grandma Fannie and Grandpa Fog and chanted:

My dearest Fog and Fannie,

You are the best grandpa and granny.

You sent me an invitation,

To share in your celebration.

But the success must really go,

To your granddaughter as you know.

She is the most amazing bug,

If she wasn't so small, I'd give her a hug.

She asked me to join you today,

And it is truly my pleasure to say,

Happy Anniversary to both of you,

And Welcome Home to Fiddle, too!

Twyla blushed as the star of the show pointed at them. She and Fiddle took a little bow and then Fiddle took her hand and held it up like she was the champion. She didn't usually get this much attention but she had to admit that it really felt good to hear the clapping and see the smiles on everyone's faces. It felt especially good when Grandpa Fog hugged her right off of her feet and Grandma Fannie kissed her softly on the forehead.

Molly sang a couple of her old standbys. She shared her brand new single, 'Magpies, Dandelions and Love' as the encore when the crowd just wouldn't stop blinking her name.

Then, as only Molly could, she blew kisses and finished the night with this final ditty.

So now I bid you all adieu.

Thanks for letting me sing for you!

Don't forget that we share this land,

We must take care of her, hand in hand.

In order to be happy and thrive,

We need to work together to stay alive!

Be good to the earth, she is our Mother,

And remember to always love each other.

Grandma Fannie memorized each word as it spilled from Molly's lips. She had always been in awe of this woman and could still not believe that she had been singing right there in front of her.

"There goes the most inspiring woman on the planet," Grandma Fannie sighed as Molly headed off towards the city on her bicycle.

"Not just because she is such a talented singer and songwriter, but for her constant caring and concern for the planet and all its creatures. She is a sister to Mother Earth."

Grandma Fannie wiped away a tear of joy as she hugged Twyla a little tighter and hummed along to her new favourite song.

No deceiving, never leaving...

This is love.

After the party, Twyla and her grandmother were snuggling on the couch waiting for the sun to come up. They were still laughing and talking about some of the highlights of the party. Twyla was feeling cozy as she pulled up the blanket almost to her little bug ears.

Mmmmmm, she thought.

She could smell the scent of the fresh grass that Grandma Fannie used to weave the blanket especially for her. She didn't want this night to end. She was so glad that the party went well, right from the moment that Grandma Fannie and Grandpa Fog realized the surprise to the last goodbye as the guests returned to their homes.

Grandpa Fog was asleep in the chair next to them and even his snoring could not slow the chatter as they talked about the party. Grandma said she was 'on cloud nine' which Twyla figured was a good thing. She didn't really know why it was this specific cloud, because hitching a ride on a cloud would be a fantasy come true, regardless of which number it was.

Twyla and Fiddle had pulled off the party of the century. From the great food, to the beautiful decorations and spectacular fireworks, the whole thing went off without a hitch. Grandma still got teary when she started to talk about the moment that surprised them all, especially Twyla, when Molly Reardon appeared out of nowhere.

"I don't know how on earth you were able to get Molly Reardon to our party," said Grandma Fannie. "That, my girl, was a real live miracle!"

"Wishes really do come true, Grandma Fannie. I wished for you to meet your idol, and I wished that Fiddle was okay, and they both came true," said Twyla. "I really am a lucky bug."

Grandma dozed off clinging tightly to her memories and her granddaughter. Twyla smiled to herself as she drifted off to sleep.

I wonder what Molly is doing around Grandma Fannie's birthday! Wouldn't it be great if they could sing a duet together? That would be a great birthday present...

The End

ACKNOWLEDGMENTS

I am so grateful to the remarkable teachers and mentors who believed in me long before I believed in myself. From Mrs. Uena Trotter in grade 5 where the spark began when she challenged the class to write a children's book, to Lesley Francis, my creative writing group facilitator and the group members that encouraged me in Edmonton, Alberta where Twyla was born. To Margaret MacPherson and Gail Sidonie-Sobat, two amazing authors who provided their expertise through the Writer's in-Residence program at Edmonton Public Library whose support helped me believe in my writing abilities and that one day she would fly.

Thank you to Roberta Della-Picca, Anna Camilleri and Wy-J Kou who provided reassurance and wisdom so that I was able to stay grounded enough to believe in myself.

My heartfelt gratitude to Cameron Montgomery and Rose Bennett at Studio Dreamshare Press for making my dream come true. I never would have believed it!

To all my family and friends who have encouraged me along the way. It takes cheerleaders to keep believing.

Especially to Tom...from the first page to the last, he was as excited about the story as anyone could be! He would prompt me-"What happens next?" Thank you for your unwavering support and helping me believe in happily ever afters.

And to my wonderful sons, Greg, and Russell, I will always love you for believing in me, too.